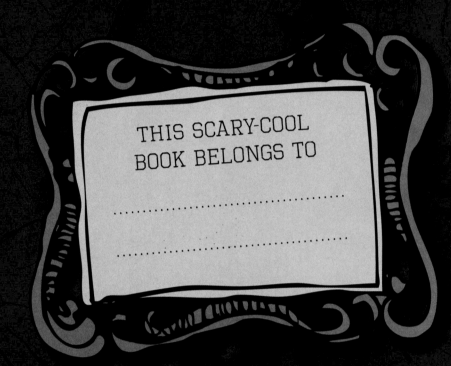

THIS SCARY-COOL
BOOK BELONGS TO

....

....

This edition published by Parragon Books Ltd in 2013 and distributed by

Parragon Inc.
440 Park Avenue South, 13th Floor
New York, NY 10016
www.parragon.com

ISBN 978-1-4723-4237-9

Printed in China

MY MONSTER LIFE

CONTENTS

A monster hello from the student bodies!

So, you're thinking about enrolling at Monster High?
Creeperific choice! It's the beast school ever—
THE place to make fiends with tons of scary-cool ghouls.

Follow us and we'll show you around … and explain how
things work. This book will take you through the whole,
horrific year. Be sure to check the Monster High noticeboard
at the beginning of each month so you can keep up with all
our comings and groanings. The board lists dates for your
die-ary, plus all kinds of notices from Headless Headmistress
Bloodgood™ (she's headless, but you'll get used to it)
and the other faculty members. Most importantly you can
see who's been voted "Student of the Month" and read up
on all their gruesome details.

There's always something going down at Monster High.
The corridors are buzzing with extra-scare-icular clubs and
societies, so whether you're into fearleading or fashion,
you'll find something that suits you.

What are you waiting for? It's time to get to grips with
un-life at the school where screams come true!

MONSTER HIGH

A Monstrous Boo Year

WHAT'S ON IN January

9th
Newspaper Club reconvenes
16th
Fearleading trials
20th
Gory Gazette bumper issue out
27th
Growl Choir first rehearsal

Welcome back students. I do hope that you are suitably relaxed after the howlidays and ready to resume your deaducation! There are many ugh-mazing events to look forward to this year. This remains a place of learning, however, so please remember that iCoffins are banned in class at all times. Anyone discovered using one during lessons will find themselves cleaning out the Pit of Fear—which is soon to be refurbished with money raised by the P.C.A. (Parent Creature Association).

Wishing you a studious year,

Headmistress Bloodgood

Creepateria Menu

Tarantula Terrine
Roast Loin of Unicorn
Steak (Bloody)

Scare-ots
Bleurgh-ccoli Spears
Claw-liflower Cheese

This year we will also be introducing a student dessert favorite to the menu every Thursday. Add your suggestions below:

....
....
....

Please note that extra-scare-ricular activities are available to all students Ms. de Nile. Zombies are therefore welcome at trials.

Mr. D'eath ⟶

FEARLEADING TRIALS

Dear wannabes,

Try-outs for my award-winning Fear Squad will take place at 5pm in the gymnasium. In case you haven't heard, I've recently steered the team to Monster Mashional victory. The standard I expect is VERY high. Due to the speed needed to make the grrrr-ade zombies need not apply.

Cleo xx

Frankie Stein™

NAME: Frankie Stein.

PET: Watzit™, my father created him in his lab for me.

STYLE: Black and white plaid, also stripes accessorized with bolts of electricity.

SCHOOL HIGHS: Helping Jackson Jekyll™ and Holt Hyde™ accept their dual personality.

SCHOOL DIES: Accidentally falling for Queen Bee Cleo's guy, Deuce, on my first day.

NOMINATED BY: Draculaura and Clawdeen Wolf.

REASON:
New year, new ghoul in school. Our GFF perfectly disembodies all the hope and excitement that we feel in January. We never know what a new year will bring at Monster High—will Heath Burns™ ever get a ghoulfriend? Will Robecca Steam's dad ever emerge from the catacombs?

It's the same with Frankie. Will her hand fly off during fearleading? Will she accidentally electrocute the entire swim team? Maybe, but whatever happens we know she'll always do everything with enthusiasm! This is one high-voltage ghoul.

NEWSPAPER CLUB:
WHO'S MADE THE FRONT PAGE?

Gory Gazette
Newbies Make a Grave Impression

Two students from out of town have made the front page this month. How eek-citing! Draculaura was first on the scene to take the ghouls' pics, but her camera isn't working properly. Every shot is a pixelated disaster!

Can you tell who is being featured? Study each snarled-up shot, then write the correct name in the caption space below each picture. Check your answers on page 69.

She'd never admit it of course, but Headmistress Bloodgood is secretly a bloodsucker for astrology! When she's sure that no one's looking, she checks out the horrorscopes in *Teen Scream* magazine. Oh my ghoul! The students would freak if they knew that the Head secretly enjoyed their favorite read! What do the scary stars have in store for you this year? Let's find out....

The Year A Head

Aquarius
January 20 – February 18
You are one of the most productive signs of the zodiac, so this year it's going to be full scream ahead with your plan to ace those Scary Aptitude Tests. With hard work and deadication your goal is achievable. Don't neglect your beast fiends however – you're going to need their support around the howliday season.

Pisces

February 19 – March 20
No one has ever accused you of being a natural at fearleading, but you're about to make your monster peers sit up and take notice. A shift in lunar activity in May creates some ughsome sporting opportunities. With all of the extra energy you'll have from your increased fitness, it's time for you to step up and help the important people in your un-life.

Aries

March 21 – April 19
You feel ready for anything this Boo Year's Day, but watch out Scaries, 2014 is going to shock your socks off! Even though you think that you're dating the monster of your dreams, by autumn this relationship will be consigned to the graveyard. Don't worry, the stars show that you'll soon be looking for a new flame to fang out with.

Taurus

April 20 – May 20
Your scarily stubborn nature and ability to focus really pay off this year when you finally get the recognition you deserve. An award or position of note is coming your way in September! At last you can believe that screams really do come true. Money's tight over the howliday season however, so stay away from the Maul!

Gemini
May 21 – June 20
This is a year for celebrations Gemacabre, so take every opportunity to party. Whether it's a ghoulfriend's sweet 1600th, a Halloween shriekfest or a weekend rave in the family crypt, you'll be the heart and soul of every festivity you attend. Your only social nightmare will happen in the spring. Beware of a prank that goes awry on April Ghoul's Day.

Cancer

June 21 – July 22
This year sees a seismic shift in your self-clawfidence. You are finally willing to embrace your freaky flaws and let others see you for your true, furbulous self! Your style will change with your attitude and come March you'll even be rocking a fangtastic new look. The timing couldn't be better—an intriguing zombie will shuffle into view mid-year.

Leo
July 23 – August 22
You're never one to stay behind the screams and so 2014 is your time to shine. Just remember, every golden ghoul needs to hone her skills before unleashing them on the monster world at large, so hold back until you're ready to reveal the high-voltage you. A haunting song in October brings back unwanted Monster High memories.

Virgo
August 23 – September 22
August will find you unleashing your inner werewolf and howling at the full moon. It's scary to move out of your comfort zone, but this wicked and wild new you is magnetic. In no time at all you'll be beating hot monsters off with a stick! Just be wary as some may find this threatening, especially those with a cursed idol to grind.

Libra
September 23 – October 22
Fur will fly in spring when you start fanging out with a familiar group of fiends. Old rivalries will surface and before you know it you'll be as tempted to flee as a vampire at a garlic harvest. It won't be easy, but you've got to dig your claws in and stay put. With patience and persistence your differences can be resolved—even when a monster diva starts throwing her weight

Scorpio

October 23 – November 21
The Boo Year's Eve celebrations were so hectic you'll be tempted to kick off 2014 with a very long rest! Don't let the gruesome grass grow under your feet. Sure, you deserve to kick back with the ghouls, but if you want to reach your potent potential this year you'll need to get those manicured claws dirty. Don't let everybody else have all the fun—grab some for yourself!

Sagittarius

November 22 – December 21
Petrifying poltergeists! 2014 is going to be an ugh-mazing year of love for Sagit-hairy-us monsters. Singletons will find themselves having scary-sweet romantic liaisons, and those already dating a ghoul or monster will settle down for a year of harmony and stability. In June someone will try to rattle your chains, but even this can't bring you down.

Capricorn

December 22 – January 19
Doors will creak open for you in 2014 and you'll find yourself drawn, like a lost spirit, into pastures new. Don't throw all the coffins out of your crypt yet, however. The months ahead will show that there are some things worth fanging on to, even if they don't reflect the new you. A highlight comes in the autumn, when you'll have a hoot at a ghostly banquet.

Make Your Own

TEAR-RIFIC TEE

Cleo traditionally holds fearleading trials in January, but sadly a dragon broke into the changing rooms over the howlidays and shredded all the spare uniforms! Luckily this wasn't all bad news. The break-in gave Cleo the inspiration to create scary-cool, slash-back tees for the squad. Here's how to make yours....

FEAR squad PRIDE

FEAR SQUAD GHOUL

- 1 old T-shirt (black is best)
- Scissors
- Piece of chalk (tailor's or craft)
- Ruler

DON'T LOSE YOUR HEAD!

Ask before taking a tee, then get an adult to help with the cutting.

HERE'S WHAT YOU DO:

1. Cut around the neck of the T-shirt to remove the collar. You can make the new neckline as wide and jagged-looking as you like.

2. Place the T-shirt face down on a table so that you're working on the back. Use chalk to draw two parallel lines down the center that are around 2 1/2 inches apart. This strip of material will become the "spine" of the tee and will always remain in place.

3. Next draw a series of horizontal lines coming out from the spine. Cut along these to create a row of "ribs." The lines should be about 3/4 inch apart. Begin the rows about 1 1/4 inches down from the neckline, ending them approximately 2 inches up from the bottom of the tee.

4. Take the scissors and cut along each line, remembering to leave the "spine" strip of material in the center intact. Take care to stop each cut around an inch away from the side seam of the T-shirt.

5. When you've finished cutting, give the T-shirt a good stretch so that the strips become more rounded and "stringy." Your fearleading tee is ready to wear!

For a killer look, wear your slashed tee over a tank in an eye-popping color like red, pink, or electric blue. Team it with leggings and you're ready to freak out in the gym. You could even cut the sleeves off to create a boxy, vest shape.

FEBRUARY

WHAT'S ON IN February

1st
Freaky February – Freaky Flaws debate

2nd
Shockey team talk and try outs

3rd
Comic Club first meeting

14th
Voltageous Valentine's Party

21st
Shockey teams announced

Be My Voltageous Valentine....

In the spirit of Freaky February (the month when students are encouraged to appreciate each others' freaky flaws) we are hoping that every student will find a partner for the Voltageous Valentine's Party. If you are still seeking a monster to complete your scary-cute couple, please write your name and iCoffin™ number below.

HEATH BURNS — TEL: 11 35 33 55
Operetta™ — Tel: 26 83 02 00
Jackson Jekyll — TEL: 11 46 76 19
Manny Taur™ – Put note in my locker. iCoffin confiscated!

Feeling Uniquely Freaky

I AM PLEASED TO ANNOUNCE THE ADDITION OF SHOCKEY TO THE SPORTS SCARE-RICULUM THIS TERM. THIS HORRIFIC TEAM SPORT HAS 11 PLAYERS, HOOKED STICKS, AND A ROCK-HARD BALL, WHICH, IN FULL FLIGHT, COULD EASILY DE-FANG A VAMPIRE. IN MY OPINION, THIS BRUTAL FORM OF EXERCISE IS JUST WHAT YOU NAMBY-PAMBY STUDENTS NEED!

I LOOK FORWARD TO ~~ENFORCING IT~~ INTRODUCING IT THIS MONTH, WITH A VIEW TO ENTERING A TEAM INTO THE INTER-SCHOOL TOURNAMENT IN MARCH. SEE YOU ON THE FIELD,

COACH IGOR

FREAKY FEBRUARY

EMBRACE YOUR FREAKY FLAWS!

Open debate and discussion on tween esteem.

featuring guest speaker Emily Anne McSharded of the Westophit Company.

Place: Main Hall
Date: February 1st
Time: 9pm

Valentine on the door

STUDENT OF THE MONTH

Draculaura™

NAME: Draculaura.

PET: Count Fabulous™, I love fanging around with my bat!

STYLE: Pink, pink, and more pink. Oh, and I love hearts, too!

SCHOOL HIGHS: Bagging the lead role in *Hamlet The Musical* after my ugh-mazing clawdition "O, woe is me, to have seen what I have seen!"

SCHOOL DIES: Fainting at the sight of Mr. Hack's blood sausages during a varsity casketball match. (Luckily Clawd Wolf™ was there to catch me.)

NOMINATED BY: Frankie Stein and Clawdeen Wolf.

REASON: No monster makes a more fitting student in February than Draculaura. Every day is Valentine's Day in Draculaura's un-life. This fearsomely friendly ghoul is crazy in love with love! She'll never give up on the idea of walking off into the sunset with the monster of her dreams, whether she's flirting with a monster who's been turned to stone by Deuce Gorgon™ or going to the Coffin Bean™ for clawfee with Heath Burns. She's known Clawd Wolf since before he was house-trained and they are currently dating, so maybe she will get the howlingly happy ending she deserves after all.

You betta treat my big bro right, sista! C x

This month the comic clubbers, led by die-hard graphics-freak Ghoulia Yelps™, have taken a lurk back at Monster High hiss-tory. Did you know that the school's unique student bodies didn't always celebrate each other's differences?

Comic Book Club

Hiss-toria

Gggggggggggrrrrrr!

We transferred from an all-vampire school. It wasn't easy....

Vampires like Bram Devein and Gory Fangtell were new to Monster High.

It can be said that the war ended here, at Monster High.

Mwah Ha Ha Ha Ha!

Euuurgh! You smell. Maybe it's time to use soap and water ... instead of your tongues.

We may have been a little rude.

We werewolves weren't any better.

This is our turf now, got it vam-poseurs?

Freaky February

Freaky February is a special time at Monster High. It's the month deadicated to appreciating one another's freaky flaws in all their glory. It's a scary-cool celebration of uniqueness! Freaky February is especially important for vampire and werewolf students—it's the one time they put aside their age-old feud and appreciate each other's qualities.

Make a list of the things that make Draculaura totally unique. Describe all her most fangtastic attributes, then turn your attention to Clawdeen. What makes the talon-ted werewolf so ugh-mazing? When you've finished draw a picture of the drop-dead gorgeous duo in action.

Draculaura is freaky-fangtastic because.....................................

....

....

....

Clawdeen is freaky-furbulous because.....................................

....

....

....

Minute Mind Mash

Draculaura is totally over-excited—it's also her birthday this month! The ghouls are making sure that she gets trick or treated with a party and a putrid pastry of a cake. Give yourself 60 seconds to look at this photo, then cover it up with a sheet of paper. Now take your chances answering the questions below.

1. Who is in the photo with Draculaura?
....

2. What is he wearing on his head?
....

3. What color is his tie?
....

4. Is the mystery boy standing on the left or the right of Draculaura?
....

5. What is he about to give the birthday girl?
....

6. How many tiers does Draculaura's cake have?
....

7. Does it have candles?
....

8. What's special about Draculaura's hair band?
....

9. Why are her shoes perfect for her birthday party?
....

10. How many earrings did you spot in the photo?
....

19

SCARY-COOL IN SCARIS

STUDENTS

Anyone interested in taking part in the Beast Cook Bake-off should report to the Home Ick rooms after school on Friday. You should by now have practiced and pawfected your revolting recipes ready for the contest. Cauldrons will be provided. Frankie Stein has kindly agreed to display her winning entry from last year - a giant gingerbread man—which will again be brought to life.

Ms. Kindergrübber

WHAT'S ON IN March

6th
Home Ick—Beast Cook Bake-off

15th-20th
Field trip to Scaris

29th
Inter-school shockey tournament

30th
Graveyard Club general pre-planting clean up

GE-OGRE-PHY FIELD TRIP TO SCARIS

ITINERARY

DAY 1
Depart from the steps of Monster High at 6am. Arrive in Scaris at 6pm.

DAY 2
Morning welcome meeting at Scaris School of Gargoyles. Afternoon free.

DAY 3
Visit to the Eiffel Terror and the Palace of Ver-sigh.

DAY 4
Trip to Scaris Fashion Week, tickets available for some shows. (These will be issued on a first come, first scared basis.)

DAY 5
Visit to leading architectural wonders of the City of Frights including Monstermartre and Notre Daaarrggghm!

DAY 6
Free day. Transportation to local shopping mauls to be arranged.

STUDENT OF THE MONTH

Rochelle Goyle™

NAME: Rochelle Goyle.

PET: Gargoyle griffin, Roux™. She was mine from the time she was hatched!

STYLE: Shades of stone and gravel gray are my favorite colors. I am also liking the pink and blue and the stripes.

SCHOOL HIGHS: Being given the positions of Howl Monitor and School Safety Monitor by the headmistress.

SCHOOL DIES: When Coach Igor is making me do swimming class. I am sinking like the stone.

NOMINATED BY: Robecca Steam, Ghoulia Yelps, and Deuce Gorgon.

REASON: We think Rochelle should be "Student of the Month" in March because we can't wait to visit her hometown of Scaris this month! Rochelle has been a rock-solid asset to Monster High since joining us from the School of Gargoyles. We can always lean on her in times of crisis and she is stone-cold serious about her role of Safety Monitor so students always feel protected in the building. We are all hoping that Rochelle will show her ghoulfriends around when we go to Scaris on the field trip. Miss Goyle knows the "City of Frights" like the back of her claw.

Scaris Fashion Week

Scaris Fashion Week is here at last! Top designer Moanatella Ghostier has supplied a stunning outfit for Rochelle and her GFFs to model. Can you sketch an ughsomely-unique Ghostier outfit for each ghoul to debut on the catwalk?

Use only your most creeperific colors, carefully putting together dresses, pants, and tops to create the pawfect look for each model. The theme for the collection is "Midnight in Scaris."

It's A
Bling Thing
Don't forget to deck your
models out in scary-cool
accessories!

23

Lost in Scaris

Scaris is an amazing place, but its dank alleys have so many twists, turns, and dead-ends, it's easy to get lost. The Monster High ghouls are on a night out with their guide, Rochelle, but she has been separated from the group. Can you help the GFFs pick their way back through the spooky streets? Follow the yellow line to reach Miss Goyle. Check the answer on page 69 if you get lost!

START

FINISH

Rochelle's been given the job of Howl Monitor! It's up to her to ensure that the students don't loiter, litter, or lay around when they should all be in class. She has issued warnings to the ten students listed below. Can you find their names in the grid? The letters you seek could be running in any direction! You'll find the answers on page 69.

N	H	Y	D	O	L	W	O	E	M	T	S	X
N	E	O	P	U	R	R	E	S	Y	O	P	H
I	P	C	L	A	D	W	L	O	S	F	O	E
E	I	F	E	T	O	R	I	L	C	O	L	A
T	R	R	C	R	H	Y	N	A	D	O	C	T
S	T	A	L	S	O	Y	E	U	E	D	N	H
E	S	S	A	T	T	O	D	S	L	U	O	B
I	I	I	W	E	I	E	O	E	D	D	M	U
K	E	M	D	U	V	E	E	H	Y	O	I	R
N	L	O	W	O	N	G	L	M	N	A	S	N
A	A	C	O	J	N	R	C	M	I	L	A	S
R	R	D	L	M	A	N	N	Y	T	A	U	R
F	O	A	F	R	A	K	I	E	U	R	S	H
O	T	S	U	L	U	M	O	R	V	O	K	T

MANNY TAUR
CLAWD WOLF
FRANKIE STEIN

HEATH BURNS
HOLT HYDE
HOODUDE VOODOO™
CLEO DE NILE™

ROMULUS
SIMON CLOPS
TORALEI STRIPE™

A mischievous kitty is about to be added to Rochelle's list. Can you locate her name in the grid? Now write it below.

....

25

MY BEAST FRIEND'S A -NORMIE-

Don't forget to pick up your frɛɛ Normiɛ Day badgɛ—availablɛ from thɛ school officɛ now. Jackson Jɛkyll

Monster High In Full Gloom

WHAT'S ON IN April

6th
Trigular calconometry review session with Lou Zarr

8th
National Normie Day

22nd-26th
Spring Break trip to Gloom Beach

24th-26th
Spirit Staff competition at Gloom Beach

Victory for Monster High!

EEEEEEK-MAIL

TO: headmistressbloodgood@monsterhigh.edu
FROM: scarym@spiritstaff
SUBJECT: Spirit Staff Competition

Dear Headmistress,
I hope you and your fiery steed are in headless good health. I would be grrrrateful if you would pass the message below to your Fear Squad and any other students who may be staying on the North Beach at Gloom Beach during Spring Break.

STUDENTS
This year's fearleading camp is again by invitation only. I shall be sending these out by iCoffin on March 14th. As reigning Spirit Staff holders and Monster Mashional champs, Monster High's Fear Squad gains an automatic bye into the competition. Normal rules apply for training, however, and the South Beach boot camp will be as fearsomely strenuous as usual. We hope to see a great Monster High turnout this year. All students are welcome to cheer on Cleo de Nile and the rest of the team as they seek to regain the title.

Scary Murphy

SPIRITS

FEAR Squad

Lagoona Blue™

NAME: Lagoona Blue.

PET: Neptuna™ the piranha. She's bite-iful!

STYLE: The clue is in the name. I like ocean blue, sea green, and wavy patterns.

SCHOOL HIGHS: Paddling Monster High to victory in the pool as captain of the swim team.

SCHOOL DIES: Drawing a picture of my underwater crush, Gillington "Gil" Webber™ in my clawculus book— then losing it!

NOMINATED BY: Draculaura, Frankie, Clawdeen, Abbey Bominable.

REASON: Lagoona should definitely be "Student of the Month" for May! She is a total Gloom Beach babe, from her weird webbed fingers to her spooktacular surfer-girl curls. Lagoona is the most fin-credible exchange student we've ever had at Monster High—besides being an ughsome aquatic athlete, she looks out for everybody 24/7. She is also doing her best to single-handedly heal saltwater/freshwater relations by dating Gil Webber.

APRIL

ON AIR

C.A. Cupid™ has a new slot on her radio show—it's a sentimental look back at some of the most monstrous student relationships at Monster High! This month she's decided to feature the aquatic ups and downs of Lagoona Blue and Gil Webber. The deadicated DJ is researching pictures from the school photo album. Can you help her piece together Lagoona and Gil's waterlogged love story? Look at the pictures, then write in your captions and speech bubbles.

C.A. Cupid Radio Show

meet me at the Fountain at 3:00

Lagoona had always liked Gil Webber....

We'll be the most fintastic parents to our egg.

They were sometimes paired together in class....

28

At Gloom Beach Gil went cold on Lagoona.

Sneaky Toralei used the Fearbook to "out" the relationship.

In the end Gil phoned his parents.

Eco-Freaks

WHAT'S ON IN **May**

21st
Spirit Rally

25th
Charity Catacombs
Creepover.

RALLY ROUND

We still need more stands for the Spirit Rally! Please write your suggestions below....

Refreshments tent filled with pumpkin patties, spooky smoothies, cotton candy, claw-fee apples, and raw steak-burgers!

Test-tube tombola

CRYPT LUCKY DIP

PLEASE TAKE A FLYER

CHARITY CATACOMBS CREEPOVER IN AID OF MSPTT

Students are cordially invited to the first annual Monster High Creepover in aid of MSPTT (the Monster Society for the Protection of Plants and Trees). This will take place on Wednesday May 25th, from 10pm until dawn.

You will need to be prepared to face whatever creatures may be lurking in the catacombs, but it's for a great cause!

Coffins provided.

For sponsorship forms please see Venus McFlytrap in the Study Howl at break times.

Venus McFlytrap™

NAME: Venus McFlytrap.

PET: Chewlian™, my snappy plant—watch your fingers!

STYLE: If it's green, I'm keen! I like to see swirly leaf patterns and tendrils of color creeping through my clothes.

SCHOOL HIGHS: Starting my eco-blog with Operetta. We're encouraging monsters to treat our world with care.

SCHOOL DIES: When my mom yelled out "Remember Venus, be a flower, not a weed" at me at the school gates.

NOMINATED BY: Lagoona, Gil, Operetta, Robecca Steam.

REASON: Who better to embody May's "Student of the Month" than Venus? She's a friend to flora and fauna everywhere! Not only did this eco-friendly ghoul help Frankie organize a fashion show to showcase designs made from recycled materials, she also writes a blog encouraging environmental awareness.

This term Venus even started a Green Party at Monster High. This ghoul really believes in screeching loud about causes she believes in. We totally admire that!

SPIRIT RALLY

SPOT THE DIFFERENCE

The Spirit Rally is one of the true highlights of the Monster High calendar. The whole school comes together at a fair to celebrate the achievements of all of the sports teams. From casketball to shockey, everyone is there! As well as admiring the Monster High trophy cabinet, the fearleading squad comes out in full force. The Rally is the ideal time to wish the physical deaducation department good luck for future competitions and tournaments.

Check out this pair of framed photos of Monster High's most sporty students. Look closely at each freaktacular detail. Can you find eight differences? Check your answers on page 69.

JUNE

WHAT'S ON IN June

9th
Mad Science Fair project set-up and test run

12th-13th
Mad Science Fair in the Great Hall

21st
Bring Your Pet To Class Day

27th-29th
Exam review with Mr. Rotter in the Study Howl

We are producing a pet page for the Monster High Fearbook. Capture your cute critter during Bring Your Pet to Class Day, then pin your pix here.
Draculaura

Rotten Review

Students,

There will be dire and deadly consequences for anyone failing their Scary Aptitude Test this year. Any student who doesn't pass will need to attend retakes over the summer with me, Mr. Rotter. Mwah ha ha ha! I will be running review sessions for anyone who feels they have fallen behind. If you are unsure whether you need to attend, take this two-minute test.

1. Aquatic creatures can be separated into two main species depending on their habitat. These are: ....
....

2. Scaris is often referred to as the City of _ _ _ _ _ _ _

3. Which animal's name comes from the Latin *furritus* which means "little thief"? ....

4. Which of these is also known as The Grim Reaper?
a. The Ferocious Farmer ☐
b. Death ☐
c. The Minotaur ☐

5. What is the highest prize awarded in the sport of fearleading? ....

6. Name a fearsome creature often found lurking under bridges: _ _ _ _ _.

Check your answers below. If you scored three or less, then attendance is strongly recommended.

ANSWERS: 1. Freshwater and Saltwater; 2. Frights; 3. Ferret; 4. b. Death; 5. Monster Mashional Champions; 6. Troll

STUDENT OF THE MONTH

Ghoulia Yelps™

NAME: Ghoulia Yelps.

_ ET: Sir Hoots A Lot™. Owls are the wisest of birds.

STYLE: This question is a little facile, but I shall attempt to answer … I enjoy wearing blood red and think my horn-rimmed glasses make quite a statement.

SCHOOL HIGHS: Leading an all-zombie dodgeball team to victory against Manny Taur, and making sure Cleo's Fear Squad video clip got millions of views so the team could go to Gloom Beach.

SCHOOL DIES: Letting myself be persuaded to swap projects with Cleo at the last Mad Science Fair. Hers was pawthetic!

NOMINATED BY: Frankie, Cleo, Draculaura, and Clawdeen.

..EASON: There are no flies on this ghoul—OK, well, maybe you will find one or two buzzing around Ghoulia's head, but we wouldn't swat her for anyone! No one really knows just how much Ghoulia does for this school. Some say she's a shadowy superhero like her comic book idol, DeadFast, but this has never been proven. One thing's for sure, her GFFs would be lost without her. Ghoulia's our go-to ghoul for homework—a techno-genius who's always there to save us when we land in fearsome trouble.

Mad Science Fair

Mad Science at Monster High is anything but dull. Lessons have seen students shrinking themselves to the size of flies and the teacher, Mr. Hackington, being attacked by just-hatched baby gargoyles during an egg-rearing project!

Mr. Hack has assigned a challenging new project this month. Each pupil has to create an invention for the annual Monster High Mad Science Fair. Feel like submitting an entry? Previous stars of the show have included science queen Ghoulia's electromagnetic pulse mega-machine and a cool gizmo that turns garbage into clean, green fuel.

Check out the zombie's projects, then create your own weird and wacky invention. Mr. Hack is counting on you to win that prize!

MAD CLUB SCIENCE

JULY

MONSTER NAME ___
SUBJECT ___

WHAT'S ON IN
July

1st–7th
Scary Aptitude Test

13th
Frightday the 13th Banquet

28th
Exam results

31st
School photos
(whole school,
class, and individual)

Last year's class photo session got somewhat out of control. Please ensure you appear in the roarditorium appropriately dressed and ready for your close-up at the times written on the chalkboard in your class.

Mr. Where

BEASTLY
EXAM TIME!

Greetings students,

I hope you have your tickets for the Frightday the 13th Banquet. If you don't come you're going to miss out, big time—the Jaundice Brothers are playing! As usual when I'm involved, the whole event will be totally golden. In my role as organizer I have elected myself Scream Queen for the night and will expect you to treat me appropriately, so do <u>NOT</u> address me unless I speak to you first! I also cannot allow any freaky fashion fails on the night.

Here's a sneak preview of my outfit. Make sure you steer well clear of similar designs! See you there!

Cleo

MONSTER HIGH

Cleo de Nile™

NAME: Cleo de Nile.

PET: Hissette™, a scary-cool Egyptian cobra.

STYLE: I am simply the most stylish student Monster High has ever seen! My favorite color is gold, worn with crypt-loads of confidence.

SCHOOL HIGHS: Leading the Monster High Fear Squad in the Monster Mashionals.

SCHOOL DIES: Accidentally sending myself to the back of the line on sales day in the Maul. Curse those cursed idols!

NOMINATED BY: Ghoulia, Deuce, Frankie, Draculaura, and Clawdeen.

REASON: This Egyptian sista is at the heart of all that happens at Monster High. Cleo was the obvious choice to be in charge of the Frightday the 13th Banquet (to mark the end of the semester). Her parties are always nights to remember! Sure, Cleo can be demanding, but she has a heart that's as golden as the rest of her. She once bought Ghoulia a first-edition *DeadFast* comic that she had always wanted! Cleo's icy exterior melts for Deuce's charms, and she has freaky flaws just like the rest of us. Did you know that she's afraid of the dark?

PICTURE DAY PICK

Picture Day is looming. It's one of the most important events in the Monster High school calendar! Each student's monstrous image is preserved for eternity (and even shown in the Fearbook), so you need to look your absolute beast. Answer YES or NO to the first question, then follow the arrows through the chart to discover whose scary-cool style you'd pick to pose in.

START

I always put on my spookiest smile for the camera.

YES → I like to check my freaky reflection before I pose.

YES → I love electrifying patterns and prints. **YES**

NO → A golden ghoul like me always flings on the bling.

NO → I look fierce in frills.

NO (from reflection) →

NO (from always put on) In a gruesome group shot, I make sure I'm at the front.

YES → My killer style features lots of snug pieces.

NO → Halter neck styles look clawsome on me.

A golden ghoul like me always flings on the bling. **YES** → Halter neck styles look clawsome on me.

I look fierce in frills. **YES** → I look creepily chic in mini-dresses.

NO (frills) **YES** →

I look creepily chic in mini-dresses. **YES** → Plaid detail shoes are frightfully pretty

I look creepily chic in mini-dresses. **NO** →

My killer style features lots of snug pieces. **YES** → I might wear shocking stockings or tights.

My killer style features lots of snug pieces. **NO** → Halter neck styles look clawsome on me.

Halter neck styles look clawsome on me. **YES** →

Halter neck styles look clawsome on me. **NO** → Any killer heel rules as long as it's black or pink.

A golden ghoul like me always flings on the bling. **NO** → Any killer heel rules as long as it's black or pink.

I might wear shocking stockings or tights. **YES** →

I might wear shocking stockings or tights. **NO** → Shoes? Hmm … monstrous metallics are my favorite.

Shoes? Hmm … monstrous metallics are my favorite. **NO** → Any killer heel rules as long as it's black or pink.

Shoes? Hmm … monstrous metallics are my favorite. **YES** →

A semi up hair-do looks hairrific.

YES →

YES

NO

YES

I'm freakily unique in quirky accessories like suspenders.

NO

YES

NO

I like shoe straps that snake eerily around my ankles.

NO

Scary-cute pigtails work for me.

YES

YES

NO

NO

My hair looks spooktacular worn long with bangs.

NO

YES

You wear high-voltage heels and spooky separates to mix up a freaky-unique style that's all your own. Ughsome accessories are your thing—you know how to wear a beastly bag, horrific hat or scary-cute suspenders to set off your outfit. You're one fierce fashionista whose stand-out style means you always shine

You'd die for Frankie's voltageous fashion flair!

Your spooky sweet smile looks great in photos and your color of choice—shocking pink—always makes an impact. For a freaky photo session you match monstrous make-up with a pair of killer heels. Dresses with fierce frills make you feel gorgeously ghoul-ie.

You think Draculaura's look is fangtastic!

You know the creepy camera loves you and you're confident that you always look ugh-mazing. For your close-up you'll be wearing something snug to show off your fearsome figure. You like wearing your hair lusciously long and spooktacularly sleek.

You admire Cleo's killer style!

SCHOOL'S OUT

Students,

I hope you enjoyed your year at Monster High, you have (as a whole) worked very hard! The summer should be a well-deserved break.

Rules:

1. Remember that even when prowling off school grounds, you represent Monster High. Please behave in a manner we can be proud of.

2. I expect you all to return in September fully rested after months sleeping in your crypts. Therefore there will be no summer reading set.

3. Next month we will be creating a memory clawllage on the wall of the creepateria so please bring in some photos of your break. I have pinned up some examples.

I look forward to seeing you all in September.

Headmistress Bloodgood

-Beastival-

THE **SCARY-COOLEST** SUMMER **FESTIVAL** EVER TAKES PLACE AT **FREAKFEST** FROM AUGUST 7TH-12TH!

This event is now sold out
To win tickets text freak477 to 999666.

ON THE PYRAMID STAGE

Jason Biter
The Jaundice Brothers
Wolf & the Wild Things

GUEST DJS INCLUDE

HOLT HYDE

Summer Scare-cation

C.A. Cupid Radio Roadshow

will be broadcasting from Skull Shores this summer so come along and join in the freaky fun!

Sneak peeks will be posted online during the trip.

Which scary-cool couple will be breaking up this summer? Continue checking in to Ghostly Gossip's blog for all the latest news over the coming month.

Robecca Steam™

NAME: Robecca Steam.

PET: My mechanical penguin, Captain Penny™. He needs a rocket pack to keep up with me!

STYLE: I call it "old school" but my friends call it "steampunk."

SCHOOL HIGHS: Helping out everyone at Monster High when Heath Burns caused a power outage. I showed them how to study without relying on technology.

SCHOOL DIES: Arriving so late for one of Cleo's creepovers that everyone was already asleep! My internal clock runs slow, you see.

NOMINATED BY: Frankie, Venus, Rochelle, and Ghoulia.

REASON: Robecca is late, a lot, due to her internal body clock malfunctioning. Despite this, the ingenious ghoul is still mostly two steps ahead of everyone else at Monster High. Her ughsome rocket boots jet-propel her up and down the howlways—we sooo want a pair of those fur-rocious rides! Robecca has many quaint, old-fashioned habits— you'll never find her looking at online videos, and she doesn't even have an iCoffin. She's a total scare-devil and a spooktacular dancer. You should see her doing robotics! Robecca deserves to be "Student of the Month" for August because, while we're all at Skull Shores, she'll spend her vacation in the catacombs searching for her lost father.
We'll miss you, Robecca!

SEPTEMBER

Film Club will be hosting a scary human movie night this month, in anticipation of next month's FrightDay the 13th celebrations.

We will be showing some terrifying films from the back catalog of Quentin Tarantula and Steven Screamberg. These are not for the faint-hearted (or those who suffer from a fear of the dark, Miss de Nile!) so please attend only if you are prepared to be scared.

Mr. Where

NB. Miss Stein—it would be helpful if you could be on hand to provide power if the projector fails again due to gargoyles chewing through wires.

WHAT'S ON IN
September
3rd
Human movie night
7th
Nominations for Howl Monitors, Prefects, and Headless Ghoul and Boy
10th
Meeting in the study howl at 6pm re: "Come To Monster High" online ad
15th-16th
Homecarnage prep weekender
16th
Homecarnage

Back to School Ghouls

We are in desperate need of extra pairs of claws to help set up and decorate the Great Hall in preparation for the Homecarnage Ball. The theme is "Screams Come True" and we are hoping to transform the space into an enormous graveyard. Please bring along any items lying around at home, such as chains, black spray, coffins, gravestones, and old skulls.

Work will begin at dawn on the 15th and will continue throughout the weekend.

See you there,

The Homecarnage Committee

MONSTER HIGH

Student Vote

DO YOU THINK HOWL MONITORS SHOULD HAVE THE RIGHT TO BANISH RULE-BREAKERS TO THE CATACOMBS AND ENFORCE DRAGON-GROOMING DUTIES?

....

....

☐ **Yes** OR **No** ☐

PLEASE DROP YOUR VOTES INTO THE COMMENTS BOX OUTSIDE THE HEADMISTRESS'S OFFICE.

STUDENT OF THE MONTH

Nefera de Nile™

NAME: Nefera de Nile.

PET: Azura™. My faithful scarab beetle brings me the sun.

STYLE: In abundance!

SCHOOL HIGHS: Putting Monster High on the map with my totally freaky fabulousness.

SCHOOL DIES: Nothing of my own making, but being stripped of my fearleading Mashional trophies was not my finest hour.

NOMINATED BY: I rule alone. I am sure the lack of nominations was due to envy or my scheming sister Cleo's interference.

REASON: OK, so I'll write this myself, but who better to explain why I deserve the title "Student of the Month"? Since its establishment, Monster High has never had a more influential, popular or successful student grace its hallowed howlways. Ask any member of the faculty and they will tell you what an intelligent and hardworking ghoul I was. I particularly excelled in dead languages, putting me in good shape for my globetrotting career as an international model.

SEPTEMBER

Comic fan Ghoulia thought it was time that everyone at Monster High saw the real Nefera de Nile! Check out this clever cartoon showing what her royal nastiness got up to at the Maul this weekend!

Comic Book Club

Bean Scare, Done That

It was time for the Fear Squad's charity fundraiser at the Maul....

Where are you ghouls going?

To the Coffin Bean, to work for free.

I hold the record for the most money raised!

Until today!

The proceeds were going to an awesome children's charity.

The challenge was on!

This will keep track of all the money we raise!

We want to get to here to beat Nefera's record.

I'll have a small sugar-free vanilla fangoccino.

The ghouls soon had their first customers....

A monster triple espresso with chocolate sprinkles....

Things were going scarily well.

Looks like your record's going to need bandages, Nefera.

I like to call this Cleo's bad luck charm.

The ghouls were on track to smash Nefera's total, until....

Doubt that!

Nefera pulled out one of her father's cursed idols.

48

Hello Halloween!

WHAT'S ON IN October

13th
Frightday the 13th
"Dare To Scare" Sleepover

26th
Pumpkin carving competition

29th
Parent-creature conferences

31st
Halloween Banquet

As I'm sure you are all aware, our spooktacularly talon-ted headmistress and her trusty steed, Nightmare, will be performing alongside other members of the National Headless Dressage Squad in an ugh-inspiring horse show at the Halloween Banquet. You are reminded that due to the danger of being trampled underhoof, pets must be left at home or kept under control during the evening.

Parent-creature conferences will take place on the evening of the 29th. Please ensure that your creators or guardians complete and send back the form, which you will find in your coffin locker during the first week of October. Attendance is compulsory and those unable to make that date will be called in at another point during the month for an appointment.

Headmistress Bloodgood

JOIN US FOR THE ANNUAL

Monster High

PUMPKIN CARVING EXTRAVAGANZA!

Pumpkins and tools provided

PRIZE for the best design

Spectra Vondergeist™

NAME: Spectra Vondergeist.

PET: Rhuen™ is my ghost ferret. He's almost as inquisitive as me!

STYLE: I've been called "a haunting beauty"—I guess my violet eyes and translucent skin are pretty unique. I love the color purple and accessorizing with chains.

SCHOOL HIGHS: Digging up scary-cool scoops. It was me that discovered the blossoming relationship between Gil and Lagoona! My research also helps me get to grips with tricky characters like Toralei.

SCHOOL DIES: Getting it wrong! *The Ghostly Gossip* outed the fact that Deuce was cheating on Cleo with Operetta—except he wasn't!

NOMINATED BY: Ghoulia.

REASON: No monster better disembodies the Halloween "Student of the Month" than Spectra. She haunts the school howls like no other student and is the go-to ghoul for behind the screams information on un-life at Monster High. Her daily *Ghostly Gossip* blog is a must-read. Sure, she sometimes gets it totally wrong in her haste to find a story, but at least she's enthusiastic! With her career goal of becoming a journalist, Spectra is also a key figure in Newspaper Club.

BEASTLY BASHES

The Monster High ghouls and guys love to party! October is the BIG month to let your fur down and have a wild time. Everybody who's anybody in school is up for freaking out at a beastly bash.

Print Squint

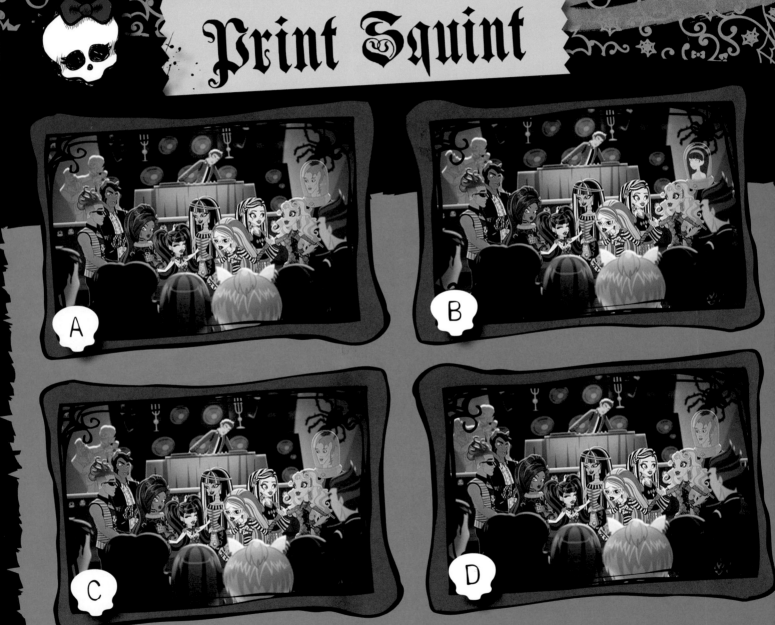

Oh My Ghoul! The Halloween Banquet was ugh-mazing this year! Cleo has had some prints done of her favorite photo showing all the gang partying the night away. The pics would have turned out great, if some gremlins hadn't got into the printer and messed up one of the shots! Look carefully. Can you tell which print is not quite the same as the others? The answer is on page 69 if you get stuck.

Now use this space to write about your two favorite monsters to mosh with at a beastly bash. Maybe they wear outfits to die for, or perhaps their monster moves are unbeatable on the dance floor? Don't forget to add photos of the ghouls in their scariest party poses!

Name: ....

A freaktacular party guest because:

....

....

....

....

....

....

....

Name: ....

A freaktacular party guest because:

....

....

....

....

....

....

HALLOWEEN PUMPKINS

with Purrsephone and Meowlody

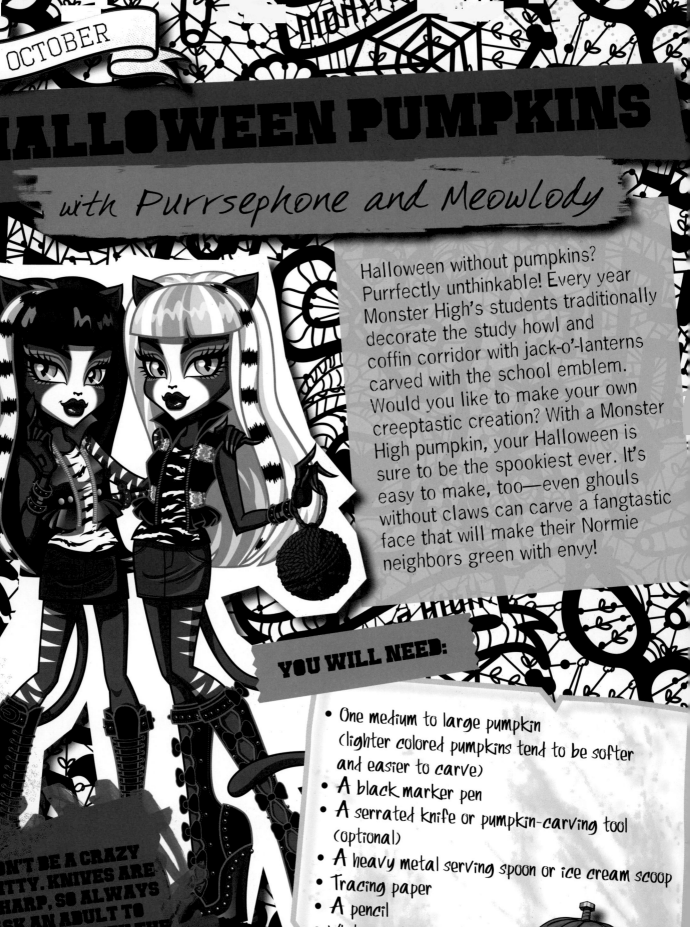

Halloween without pumpkins? Purrfectly unthinkable! Every year Monster High's students traditionally decorate the study howl and coffin corridor with jack-o'-lanterns carved with the school emblem. Would you like to make your own creeptastic creation? With a Monster High pumpkin, your Halloween is sure to be the spookiest ever. It's easy to make, too—even ghouls without claws can carve a fangtastic face that will make their Normie neighbors green with envy!

YOU WILL NEED:

- One medium to large pumpkin (lighter colored pumpkins tend to be softer and easier to carve)
- A black marker pen
- A serrated knife or pumpkin-carving tool (optional)
- A heavy metal serving spoon or ice cream scoop
- Tracing paper
- A pencil
- White card
- Scissors
- Sticky tape
- A small candle

DON'T BE A CRAZY KITTY. KNIVES ARE SHARP, SO ALWAYS ASK AN ADULT TO HELP YOU WITH THE CARVING STAGES.

1. Start by cutting a circle around the stem of the pumpkin. Draw a circle with the marker pen, then ask your adult to carve it out. Tell them to place the knife at a 45° angle as they cut so the lid will have a ledge to rest on. (If you cut straight down the lid will drop inside the pumpkin!)

2. Clean out the pumpkin using the ice cream scoop or heavy spoon. Scrape it as smooth as possible so that it will reflect the light from the candle when it's finished.

3. Trace the template above onto a sheet of white card. Use the scissors to carefully cut out the black shapes. These are the areas that will be cut out of the pumpkin.

4. Tape the template onto the pumpkin and use a black marker to trace the carving lines. Now remove the template.

5. Ask your adult helper to carve the pumpkin using the serrated knife in a sawing motion or a special pumpkin carving tool.

6. Clean away any mess, then put your lit candle inside the pumpkin and place the lid on top. Get ready to freak out anyone brave enough to visit your crypt!

Ghouls' Night Out

NOVEMBER

Create Account | Sign In

WWW.MONSTERHIGH.COM

Video **Share** | MONSTER HIGH 🔍

COME TO MONSTER HIGH

Bloodgood to head Headless Equestrian team

De Nile's squad triumphs again

Coming Soon—Monster High's Online Brochure.

WHAT'S ON IN
November

4th
"Fashion Entrepreneurs meet the Maul"
Visit the Maul to meet and talk with major monster retailers.

17th
Ogre Achievement Awards

21st
Chess Club canceled due to annual charity Zombie Lurch-out

30th
"Come To Monster High" video clip entries must be edited and submitted for viewing by the judging panel by this date.

November Nights

"Urrrgh. Bleeurgh. oogggg.yuggg aaahh."

Translation: You are cordially invited to join us for the 666th annual Zombie Lurch-out. This is to protest against the unbreakable glass ceiling for most white-collar zombie workers.

If you are planning to video a clip for the "Come to Monster High" online brochure (going live on our website in December), you will need to work hard this month. Students who missed the meeting held in September regarding requirements should understand that the idea is to offer prospective pupils a colorful and lively look at school life from a student's point of view. The state have said that admission figures have a real bearing on funding, so the aim is to attract lots of new students for 2015.

Remember:

- Your clip should last no longer than three minutes.
- You should obtain written consent to film students before including them in your movie.
- Please steer clear of the creepateria at lunch times. It annoys the kitchen staff and we really don't need lingering shots of raw steak fillets.

Clawdeen Wolf ™

NAME: Clawdeen Wolf.

PET: Crescent™ the cat.

STYLE: Furrociously fierce. We're talking big hair, gold jewelry, animal prints, and heels so high I can almost touch the moon I'm howling at.

SCHOOL HIGHS: Catwalkin' on the wild side during last year's fashion show. I really let my fur down—the audience loved me!

SCHOOL DIES: Having to sit out the last theater production in a wheelchair because Cleo and I fought too savagely for the main part.

NOMINATED BY: Frankie, Clawd, Draculaura, and Howleen.

REASON: What can we say about Clawdeen? She's a sassy werewolf with a whole lot of attitude. Firstly, she's super-athletic—is there any other ghoul in school who could rock a pair of killer heeled boots on the soccer field and beat Heath Burns in track? Nuh-uh! Secondly, she's fiercely loyal and has always got her GFFs' backs, even if that means squaring up to her big brother Clawd in order to warn him off hurting Draculaura. Thirdly, this ghoul is a die-hard fashionista who always looks immaculate from the tips of her gold-ringed ears to the ends of her pawfectly-manicured claws. Clawdeen's look just screams self-confidence.

Fierce Fashion Show

The Fierce Fashion Show is the highlight of the month for anyone who's anyone in school! Monster High's Fashion Entrepreneur's Club always attends in full force. Clawdeen Wolf, the school's fiercest fashionista, never misses a meeting.

Clawdeen can't wait to get started on her designs for the show. All she needs now is some monstrous inspiration! Can you help her put together a mood board for an ugh-mazing new collection? Use these pages to stick in, scribble, and sketch all of your ideas. What would you like to see the Monster High ghouls wearing next year? Tape in scraps of fabric or wrapping paper, cut freaky-fabulous photos out of magazines, and sketch spooky ideas to create a dead cool theme. Get styling!

Great Balls of Fire

Holt Hyde sets the decks on fire with his scary-cool mixes! Operetta's helping the hottie compile his playlist for next month's Dance of the Dead Disco. Wanna see it? Unscramble the anagrams below to reveal each track. If you get stuck, use the list on the facing page to help you unravel each song title. And look at the artists' names for a clue! When you've cracked each track name, write it on the playlist. Check your answers on page 69.

1. RIEEE NEAMIE BY **JASON BITER**

2. TIEB EM BEYAM BY **SCARY RAH JEEPERS**

3. GELSIN MOBSIZE (TUP A IRNG NO TI) BY **BEETLEBOUNCÉ**

4. LOUGH RIGL LETSY BY **PSYCHOTIC**

6. EW EAR VEERN REVE GANGFIN TOU THREEGOT BY **TERROR SWIFT**

8. EH LFWO BY **SHRIEKEERA**

7. TUJS HET YAW EW WHOL BY THE **JAUNDICE BROTHERS**

9. RICHELL BY **FRIGHTFUL JACKSON**

10. HET FAMEROSE MOTHANP OF ETH ARDRE ITERIX BY CRSSEN

Dance of the Dead Playlist

1: ....

2: ....

3: ....

4: ....

5: ....

6: ....

7: ....

8: ....

9: ....

10: ....

- Ghoul Girl Style
- Monsterazzi
- He Wolf
- Chiller
- Bite Me Maybe
- We Are Never Ever Fanging Out Together
- Single Zombies (Put a Ring On It)
- Eerie Meanie
- Just the Way We Howl
- The Fearsome Phantom of the Opera Theme (Remix)

Bonus track!

Can you think up a bonus track for Operetta to add to the playlist?

....

DECEMBER

WHAT'S ON IN December

7th
Howliday menu cook-up with Ms. Kindergrübber

12th
Dance Of The Dead disco

18th and 19th
"Boo Year, Boo You"
Monster makeover, beauty and fitness workshop with Draculaura and Clawdeen Wolf

21st-24th
Ski and Snowboard long weekend trip to the mountains

Pre-ski Fitness with Abbey

First three weeks of December, Mondays, Wednesdays, and Fridays at noon—meet at main entrance.

Including:

- Ice-skating on the frozen-over swimming pool
- Circuit training in the walk-in freezers
- Forest trekking
- Do not be being late because is most rude and we will be starting without you.
- Bring own yak milk for thirst.

LET IT SNOW

Boo Year, Boo You!

Wanna look drop-dead gorgeous next year? Let Monster High's most ughsome twosome show you how. We are holding style and beauty workshops after school in the bell tower on December 18th and 19th. We'll talk you through the best new beauty products from top lines like Fierce & Flawless, and overhaul your style so you can stalk into 2015 looking spooktacular. Clawd Wolf will be on hand with fitness tips to help you feel furbulous, too.

Please attach a recent photo of yourself and a picture of the kind of look you're hoping to achieve (right). Thanks.

Draculaura and Clawdeen

Before

After

MONSTER HIGH

Abbey Bominable™

NAME: Abbey Bominable.

PET: My baby woolly mammoth is being called Shiver.

STYLE: I am wearing the ice-blue and the fur of course, but also I have ice crystal necklace which is keeping the temperature around me to be freezing, like in my mountain home.

SCHOOL HIGHS: I am sometimes giving that bully Manny Taur a taste of his own medicine with my strength.

SCHOOL DIES: When I was spending all the days tied to Frankie because she is not understanding my way of talking and I am upsetting her. Now we are good ghoulfriends so is all OK.

NOMINATED BY: Frankie, Lagoona, and Draculaura.

REASON: It is easy to mistake Abbey's blunt manner for rudeness, but if you just take some time to fang out with her, you'll find out that she is a kind, sensitive ghoul who gives good advice. Besides her bbbrrrrilliant style (you can make anything look good when you're that tall) Abbey is great to have around because she can do stuff like make slushies from the gruesome juice machine and cool off Heath Burns when he's getting hot under the collar. This month Abbey is leading an extra-scare-icular trip to her own mountain so we can all practice snowboarding. How scary-cool is that!

Date Dilemma

Abbey hasn't yet found a date for this month's Dance of the Dead. Now she's starting to freak out! Her GFFs have set up a speed-dating (or "hurry-up-dating" as Abbey calls it) event to help her bag a monster for the evening. Read what each one has to say for himself, then draw lines to match the notes to the names at the bottom of the page. Answers on page 69!

A

WELL HELLO GHOULFRIEND, YOU'RE LOOKING PRETTY HOT FOR ONE SO COLD! HOW'D YOU LIKE ME TO TAKE YOU TO THE DANCE OF THE DEAD? YOU'D BE HEAD AND SHOULDERS ABOVE THE DANCE FLOOR CROWD SO AT LEAST I'D GET TO SEE YOU FROM MY DJ BOOTH. I'VE BEEN SINGLE SINCE SPLITTING FROM HOTTIE FRANKIE STEIN. STICK WITH ME AND WE'LL SET THE SCHOOL ON FIRE!

B

I just came along with a friend, to see what's what really, I've got casketball practice in a minute, so I gotta go and anyway, I'm kinda dating this cute pink-wearing vampire.

C

A DATE? THIS IS WHAT YOU'RE DOING SITTING HERE? I WONDERED WHY THERE WAS AN EMPTY TABLE AND A HUGE LINE OF MONSTERS. LISTEN, YOU'RE KINDA COOL AND EVERYTHING, BUT MY GHOULFRIEND WOULD UNLEASH A THOUSAND EVIL CURSES ON ME IF I EVER CHEATED ON HER.

D

Wow, oh. I can't believe I'm here. at this event. with you and. like. this isn't normally the kind of thing I get to do. but ever since Frankie brought me to life as her fake boyfriend I've been looking for a creeperific ghoul to hang out with. can you pick me. pleeeease?

E

HEY GHOUL, YOU'RE LOOKING SCARY-COOL. WANT SOME HOT STUFF TO WARM THE PLACE WHERE YOUR ICY HEART SHOULD BE? IF SO, CALL OFF YOUR SEARCH. I AM THE HOTTEST MONSTER AT MONSTER HIGH. I'M ALSO THE FASTEST. WHAT? CLAWDEEN BEAT ME? THAT'S JUST A RUMOR! ANYWAY, DON'T BE AN ICE QUEEN, LET THE MOST UGHSOME MONSTER IN SCHOOL THAW YOU OUT!

F

ughghhh, eerrrrr, yugggg, uggggggg, eeeeeergh, Ghoulia, ughhhhh, arrghhhh, eeeeeerm.

CLAWD WOLF

HOODUDE VOODOO

DEUCE GORGON

HOLT HYDE

HEATH BURNS

SLOMAN "SLO MO" MORTAVITCH

Hey ghoulfriend! The clock is ticking toward midnight and the end of another clawsome year. We can't wait to find out what spooktastic shocks and creeperific surprises the next one has in store for Monster High! Use this page to write down all your boo year wishes—from making new fiends to learning a scary-cool skill, or throwing an ughsome party. Here's hoping all your screams come true!

GOODBYE FROM THE HIGH

MONSTER HIGH

PAGE 10

NEWSPAPER CLUB: WHO'S MADE THE FRONT PAGE?

Rochelle Goyle and Abbey Bominable

PAGE 19

MINUTE MIND MASH

1. Clawd Wolf
2. Sunglasses
3. Blue
4. On the left
5. Pink roses
6. Three
7. No
8. It says her age on it—1600
9. They match her cake in color and design
10. Three, including Clawd's.

PAGE 24

LOST IN SCARIS

PAGE 25

HOWL MONITOR'S WARNING WORDSEARCH

N	H	Y	D	O	L	W	O	E	M	T	S	X
N	E	O	P	U	R	R	E	S	Y	O	P	H
I	P	C	L	A	D	W	L	O	S	F	O	E
E	I	F	E	T	O	R	I	L	C	O	L	A
T	R	R	C	R	H	Y	N	A	D	O	C	T
S	T	A	L	S	O	Y	E	U	E	D	N	H
E	S	S	A	T	T	O	D	S	L	U	O	B
I	I	I	W	E	I	E	O	E	D	D	M	U
K	E	M	D	U	V	E	E	H	Y	O	I	R
N	L	O	W	O	N	G	L	M	N	A	S	N
A	A	C	O	J	N	R	C	M	I	L	A	S
R	R	D	L	M	A	N	N	Y	T	A	U	R
F	O	A	F	R	A	K	I	E	U	R	S	H
O	T	S	U	L	U	M	O	R	V	O	K	T

The mischievous kitty is MEOWLODY

PAGES 32-33

SPIRIT RALLY SPOT THE DIFFERENCE

PAGE 52

PRINT SQUINT

B is different

PAGES 62-63

GREAT BALLS OF FIRE

1. EERIE MEANIE by Jason Biter
2. BITE ME MAYBE by Scary Rah Jeepers
3. SINGLE ZOMBIES (PUT A RING ON IT) by Beetlebouncé
4. GHOUL GIRL STYLE by Psychotic
5. MONSTERAZZI by Lady Ghoula
6. WE ARE NEVER EVER FANGING OUT TOGETHER by Terror Swift
7. JUST THE WAY WE HOWL by the Jaundice Brothers
8. HE WOLF by Shriekeera
9. CHILLER by Frightful Jackson
10. THE FEARSOME PHANTOM OF THE OPERA THEME (REMIX) by Crescenda von Hammerstone

PAGE 66

DATE DILEMMA

A. Holt Hyde
B. Clawd Wolf
C. Deuce Gorgon
D. HooDude Voodoo
E. Heath Burns
F. Sloman "Slo Mo" Mortavitch